I0571117

Lost and Found

a stage play

Alyssa Ahle

For Dr. Michelle Miller-Day and Deb Marley
Thank you for helping make this play a reality

"*Lost and Found* is an actor's play...ultimately Ahle, Marley, and their cast are able to grab the audience's attention right from the start, pick up their sympathy and genuine investment along the way, and finish by offering the greatest gift a play can give its viewers: a deeper understanding of the complexity of human relationships."

- Excerpt from a review of *Lost and Found's* workshop production, 2017, by Parker Danowski

ALYSSA AHLE

Original Cast – Workshop Production 2017
Performed at the Chance Theater

Produced by Dr. Michelle Miller-Day & Alyssa Ahle
Directed by Deb Marley

DEPDENDENCE – Sarah Kaino
DESIRE – Meir Parent
DR. ADAMS/BARTENDER/
HOST/WAITER – Jolynn Jones
GRIEF – Brad Painter
GUARDED – Nathan Famador
HEARTACHE – Kendyl Grbac
LOST – Cody Aaron Hanify
SILENCED – Maxie Lankalingam
SIMON – Jeffrey Mutschler
UNREQUITED LOVE – Laruen Lundeen

Original Cast – Workshop Reading 2016
Performed at Chapman University

DEPDENDENCE – Lizzy Mosher
DESIRE – Randy Wuske
DR. ADAMS/BARTENDER/
HOST/WAITER – Ruth Burgess
GRIEF – Adron Duell
GUARDED – Parker Danowski
HEARTACHE – Hannah Zickel
LOST – Teddy MacKay
SILENCED – Sarah Kaino
SIMON – Austin Sauer
UNREQUITED LOVE – Talia Goodman

1

Lost and Found Character Breakdown

DEPENDENCE, A young woman who constantly handcuffs herself to people.

DESIRE, A young man blinded by love; tries to hide his visual impairment.

DR. ADAMS, A doctor who runs a group therapy session for people suffering from love's emotional scars. Role can be male or female, young or old. Actor will also play the roles of the restaurant staff (i.e. Bartender, Host, & Waiter).

GRIEF, A young man who sees and interacts with his deceased wife and carries her around in a collapsible chair.

GUARDED, A young man with obsessive compulsive disorder (OCD) who is terrified of catching the love bug; protects himself by wearing medical gloves and a medical mask.

HEARTACHE, A young woman who suffers from a broken heart and walks with a cane.

LOST, A young man who misplaced his heart.

SILENCED, A young woman who wears duct tape over her mouth.

UNREQUITED LOVE, A young woman who carts around her old crushes in a wagon.

SIMON, The young man currently situated in Unrequited Love's wagon. Provides comic relief.

SETTING:
Suburbia. The time of year is early December. Outside temperature is mid-60's Fahrenheit, or light jacket weather.

TIME:
The events of the play occur over the course of one evening.

LOST AND FOUND

Act I, Scene 1

Lights fade up on the stage. Eight folding chairs are arranged in a semi-circle facing the audience. A couple stage lights are arranged in the form of a person's shadow onstage to suggest that Dr. Adams is sitting downstage, opposite the chairs. Dr. Adams is not visible to the audience. Nine people enter from offstage. We begin to notice odd characteristics about them. Desire wears sunglasses inside. Unrequited Love tows a wagon behind her with a young man sitting inside it. Silenced has a piece of duct tape over her mouth. Dependence has a pair of handcuffs secured to her arm. Guarded wears a medical mask and medical gloves. Grief brings in an extra chair with him, setting it up next to his seat. Heartache supports herself with a cane. Lost is the only one without a physical prop. They take their seats. Dr. Adams speaks in a voiceover, addressing the characters seated onstage.

DR. ADAMS: Now that everyone's here we can begin. Dependence, please start.

DEPENDENCE: (*Stands.*) My name is Dependence, and it's been three months since I've had a second date with anyone. (*Sits.*)

LOST: (*Stands.*) My name is Lost, and it's been a year since I've had a second date with anyone. (*Sits.*)

UNREQUITED LOVE: (*Stands.*) My name is Unrequited Love, and it's been four months since I've had a second date with anyone. (*Sits.*)

HEARTACHE: (*Uses her cane to help herself stand up.*) My

4

name is Heartache, and it's been two and a half years since I've had a second date with anyone. (*Sits.*)

DESIRE: (*Stands.*) My name is Desire, and it's been eight months since I've had a second date with anyone. (*Sits.*)

GUARDED: (*Stands, speaking through his mask.*) My name is Guarded, and it's been six months since I've had a second date with anyone. (*Sits.*)

SILENCED: (*Stands. Peels the duct tape off.*) My name is Silenced. It's been five months since I've had a second date with anyone. (*Puts the tape back over her mouth and sits down.*)

GRIEF: (*Stands.*) My name is Grief, and it's been seven years since I've had a second date with anyone. (*Sits.*)

DR. ADAMS: Grief, I see you've brought Caitlin again today. You know, anyone is welcome at these sessions, but does she always want to be here?

GRIEF: (*Indicates to the empty chair beside him.*) Oh, she doesn't mind. She likes hearing everyone's stories.

DR. ADAMS: Okay then, as long as she's comfortable with it. Alright, now—

(*Simon leans forward and snaps his fingers. All the characters onstage, except for him, freeze instantly.*)

SIMON: (*Speaks in an aside to the audience.*) Hang on. I'm not one for throwing the audience into a scene without

5

warning, so here's my good deed for the day. (*Takes out a clipboard with notes. He can even get out and strut about the stage.*) Okay so basically this little rendezvous is a group therapy session that meets once a week. Each character's got some emotional scar they like to pretend they don't have. Personally, I think I'm supposed to be a metaphorical symbol of Unrequited Love's emotional baggage. I sit here in a child-sized wagon and represent her problems. So that's all I got for right now. I'll get back to you later.

(*Simon snaps his fingers and resumes his position in the wagon. The other characters come back to life.*)

DR. ADAMS: —Who would like to start us off tonight?
  (*Beat. Everyone hopes she won't pick them.*)
Grief?

(*Everyone else is visibly relieved.*)

GRIEF: Well I thought about what you said last week, about putting ourselves outside our comfort zone, so last night I went out and saw a movie.

DR. ADAMS: And how did that go?

GRIEF: It was all right. I panicked when my date picked a rom-com. But it was actually pretty good. We both loved it.

DESIRE: Did you say we?

(*Dependence gleefully claps her hands while everyone else leans forward.*)

DEPENDENCE: Grief had a movie date!

UNREQUITED LOVE: (*Excitedly.*) What's her name? What's her name?

GRIEF: (*Holds up his hands.*) Hey, hey. Don't start. (*Indicates to the empty chair.*) I took Caitlin, okay?

HEARTACHE, DEPENDENCE, GUARDED, UNREQUITED LOVE, DESIRE, & LOST: Oh.

DR. ADAMS: Grief, when I suggested that you do something outside your comfort zone, I was more so leaning towards the idea of you doing it by yourself, or maybe with...somebody else?

GRIEF: Oh.

> (*Dependence leans over to Desire and handcuffs herself to him.*)

DR. ADAMS: For example, can you recall the last time you went to the movies by yourself?

GRIEF: You mean since Caitlin...well, I don't know. She still comes with me everywhere.

DESIRE: Dr. Adams. Dependence handcuffed herself to me.

DEPENDENCE: Sorry! I'll unlock them in a minute.

DR. ADAMS: (*In a warning tone.*) Dependence.

DEPENDENCE: Or...I could just unlock them right now? (*Unlocks herself from Desire.*)

DR. ADAMS: Going back to the issue at hand...Can someone suggest another activity that'll ease Grief out of his comfort zone?

DESIRE: You could go out for coffee?

GRIEF: Hate coffee.

DEPENDENCE: Outdoor concert?

GRIEF: Too crowded.

HEARTACHE: Go dancing?

GRIEF: Two left feet.

UNREQUITED LOVE: What about mini golf? It's always fun with a group.

GUARDED: Oh, I vote mini golf.

DEPENDENCE: Me too!

DR. ADAMS: Grief? How would your two left feet feel about mini golf?

GRIEF: I guess I'll try it this weekend.

DR. ADMAS: Great! We'll look forward to hearing about it next week. Now, let's move on to someone who hasn't talked in a while. Silenced, how do you feel about sharing?
    (*Silenced looks up in a panic and shakes her head fast.*)
Silenced, no one is required to share, but I encourage you to

try tonight. We're all here to support you. Isn't that right everyone?

(*The group agrees with nods and vocal yeses.*)

GRIEF: You got this.

(*Dependence leans over and handcuffs herself to Desire again.*)

UNREQUITED LOVE: You could start with the highlight of your week...?

SILENCED: (*Peels off the duct tape.*) Well I um, adopted a dog from the shelter.

DEPENDENCE & UNREQUITED LOVE: Awwww.

DR. ADAMS: And what kind of...
(*Silenced hurriedly puts the tape back over her mouth and looks down.*)
Well that's a good start for now.

DESIRE: Dr. Adams. Dependence did it again!

DEPENDENCE: Ah sorry I'm sorry. (*Unlocks the hand--cuffs.*)

(*Desire makes the person sitting on his other side switch seats with him.*)

DR. ADAMS: (*Clears throat loudly.*) Lost. We haven't heard from you yet. How was your day?

LOST: It was fine.

DR. ADAMS: Lost, fine is a word you use when you mean the exact opposite. Like awful or painful.

LOST: No, I mean, it was fine.

DR. ADAMS: Lost. You said it again.
> (*Everyone in the semi-circle laughs, except for Lost and Simon.*)

Lost, I think that— (*Dr. Adams' cell-phone beeps.*)

DESIRE: Is something wrong?

DR. ADAMS: Oh no.

UNREQUITED LOVE: Dr. Adams, are you on call tonight?

DR. ADAMS: I told my staff to call only in the case of an emergency. There must be one. I'm sorry, I have to cancel tonight's session.

> (*Everyone reacts differently. Some are upset. Some are quite relieved.*)

DEPENDENCE: What? We just got here.

DR. ADAMS: I'm very sorry everyone; it seems that the universe has other plans for us tonight. Make sure to grab all your things. I will see you next week.

Act I, Scene 2

(*Everyone is gathered outside the building where the group therapy sessions take place, not really wanting to leave. There's a door behind them to represent the building's entrance and a bench near it. Lost and Dependence are sitting on the bench.*)

DESIRE: So this sucks.

DEPENDENCE: Now what? We just leave?

UNREQUITED LOVE: I don't know. It doesn't seem right to just go home early.

HEARTACHE: Yeah, we didn't drive all the way here for nothing.

(*Dependence gets up from her seat to wander aimlessly, leaving her jacket on the bench.*)

UNREQUITED LOVE: Well, we could all grab a drink somewhere. Anyone know a good place?

GRIEF: Giuliano's is only a few blocks away.

(*Dependence begins to inch towards Grief with her handcuffs.*)

UNREQUITED LOVE: That new Italian place?

GRIEF: That's the one.

HEARTACHE: I ate there the other day. It's really good.

UNREQUITED LOVE: Uh, Grief... (*Points to Dependence, who is about to handcuff herself to him.*)

GRIEF: Hey! (*Dodges the handcuffs, but Dependence is persistent.*) Stop it!

DEPENDENCE: (*Chases Grief around the stage as he holds onto Caitlin's chair.*) Hold still!

GRIEF: No way! (*Jumps into the audience, making his escape.*) Not happening!

DEPENDENCE: (*Jumps into the audience, following Grief.*) Get back here!

GRIEF: Never!

> (*The other characters watch as Dependence and Grief exit. Some laugh at what just happened, others don't think it's that funny.*)

HEARTACHE: (*Laughing.*) Well he's done for.

GUARDED: I'm gonna go help him. (*Exits via the audience.*)

> (*Silenced looks at the others, and then follows Guarded.*)

UNREQUITED LOVE: Should we go after them?

DESIRE: Nah. Grief's attachment to Caitlin will scare Dependence off.

HEARTACHE: Well, Giuliano's still sounds like a good idea. Anyone want to join me?

UNREQUITED LOVE: Sounds lovely.

DESIRE: Sure.

HEARTACHE: Great. You can all follow me in your cars.

DESIRE: Actually um, I'm gonna walk there, since it's just a few blocks away.

HEARTACHE: Oh well... (*Indicates to the cane she's leaning on.*) I don't know if walking's a good idea for me. Plus, it'll take me awhile to get there.

DESIRE: Endorphins are always good for the body. Maybe the walk will make you feel better.

HEARTACHE: (*Hesitates and then shrugs.*) Sure, why not? Can't get any worse than I already am.

DESIRE: (*Offers his arm to her.*) Here. You can still show me where the restaurant is.

HEARTACHE: Oh, fancy.

DESIRE: Shall we?

HEARTACHE: Yes let's.
(*Heartache takes Desire's arm, and then looks back at the others. Lost is fiddling with his shoe. Unrequited Love is trying to pull her wagon, but it's slow-going.*)
See you two there.

(*Heartache and Desire exit together. Unrequited Love watches them leave. Then she turns and sees Lost, who is still sitting on the bench. Lost doesn't seem to notice Unrequited Love, still fiddling with one of his shoes.)*

UNREQUITED LOVE: Lost? Are you going too?

LOST: (*Looks up at Unrequited Love as if he's seeing her for the first time.*) I guess.

UNREQUITED LOVE: You can ride with me. We'll beat everyone there and be heroes.

LOST: (*Stands. Indicates to the wagon behind Unrequited Love.*) Um, who is that?

(*Simon sits in the wagon reading a magazine.*)

UNREQUITED LOVE: Oh, that's Simon. I asked him out on a date in college, but he turned me down and hooked up with my roommate instead.

LOST: Ouch.

UNREQUITED LOVE: Not really. Well, I mean it did hurt a lot, but maybe if I try hard enough something will... (*Looks away, noticing Dependence's jacket on the bench.*) Hey, isn't that Dependence's jacket? (*Leans down and picks it up.*)

LOST: She must've left it by accident.

UNREQUITED LOVE: Who knows where she's gone with Grief? I'll grab it. I can always give it to her next week.

(*Unrequited Love places the jacket in the wagon with*

Simon. As she turns away, Simon snaps his fingers.
Unrequited Love and Lost freeze.)

SIMON: Come on. It's crowded enough in here. (*Throws the*
jacket out of the wagon, hesitates, and then picks it back up.)
Although I couldn't call myself a resourceful person unless I
went through the pockets and looked for loose change.

(*Simon snaps his fingers and the scene resumes.*)

UNREQUITED LOVE: My car's this way.

(*They both start to walk towards her car. Lost notices*
Unrequited Love is struggling with the wagon.)

LOST: Do you need some...?

UNREQUITED LOVE: Yes please.

LOST: (*Helps push the wagon from behind, surprised at how*
heavy it is.) Look, um Unrequited Love is it? I try not to judge
people's life choices, but how—(*Grunts.*)—Do you live if you
have to carry him around all the time?

UNREQUITED LOVE: Oh, I don't carry him around all the
time, just on Mondays. On Tuesdays, I carry around David,
my high school crush. I always wanted him to ask me to a
school dance, but he never did. Just wasn't his type I guess.
(*Beat.*) I still think about him.

LOST: I probably shouldn't ask about the other days of the
week, should I?

(*They arrive at Unrequited Love's car.*)

UNREQUITED LOVE: Here we are.

(*Unrequited Love unlocks the car. She and Lost try to lift Simon out of the wagon, struggling. Simon makes a scene of refusing their help, getting up out the wagon by himself and sitting in the backseat.*)

LOST: Is it me or is he heavier than I would've expected?

UNREQUITED LOVE: It's not you. Metaphorical symbols weigh more than the average human being.

LOST: Learn something new every day.

(*Lost and Unrequited Love put the wagon in the trunk and then get in the front of the car. They both buckle up.*)

UNREQUITED LOVE: So, what's your problem Lost?

LOST: (*Holds up his hands.*) What, with you? No problem at all.

UNREQUITED LOVE: Sorry, I mean why'd you join the therapy group? You never share much at meetings and I thought if we were alone, you might tell me.

LOST: (*Indicates to Simon in the backseat.*) We're not exactly alone.

UNREQUITED LOVE: Oh, don't mind him.

LOST: Well...I lost the love of someone I was in a relationship with. That's all.

(*Unrequited Love nods and starts the car. A love song comes on the radio. Lost reacts.*)
Oh no.

UNREQUITED LOVE: (*Turns off the car.*) You okay? Did you forget something?

LOST: No, it's just—(*Indicates to the radio, not sure how to explain that love songs make him uncomfortable.*)—The song that was playing...

UNREQUITED LOVE: Not a fan?
      (*Lost shakes his head, relieved he won't have to explain himself.*)
Oh that's okay. I've got a whole playlist of other songs we can listen to. (*Takes out her phone and scrolls through it.*) Let me see, I've got Love is a Battlefield, Stop In The Name of Love, So Much In Love, When A Man Loves a Woman, It Must Have Been Love, Love Me Do, You Can't Hurry Love—

(*As Unrequited Love is speaking, Lost looks more and more uncomfortable, till he finally unbuckles his seatbelt and tries to open the passenger side door, but it's locked.*)

LOST: I—I need air. Can you unlock—?

UNREQUITED LOVE: —What? Oh yeah. (*Unlocks her car.*)
      (*Lost opens the car door and leans out, breathing heavily.*)
Are you okay?

LOST: Yeah just give me a sec.

UNREQUITED LOVE: What? Do love songs make you sick or something?

17

LOST: No, it's just that the lyrics inspire a sort of panic in my chest.

UNREQUITED LOVE: Maybe we should just skip my playlist; it's got mostly love songs.

LOST: (*Brings himself back into the car, closing the car door.*) Okay I'm good...I'm sorry.

UNREQUITED LOVE: I think we'll stick to the radio then.

(*Lost re-buckles his seatbelt. Unrequited Love turns the car back on. We hear the artist's voice continue to sing the love song on the radio. Simon can sing along with the song if he so chooses.*)

Act I, Scene 3

(*Guarded and Silenced return from offstage, panting with exhaustion. They are in the opposite corner of the stage to show they are somewhere far from the therapy building.*)

GUARDED: (*Takes his mask off to catch his breath.*) Dependence and Grief may have issues, but man they're fast. I give up. I need orange slices and air. And water. In that order.

SILENCED: (*Rips off her duct tape.*) Out of shape. So...so out of shape.

GUARDED: Hey. (*Gasp.*) You're talking. (*Gasp.*)

SILENCED: No I'm not. (*Quickly replaces the duct tape over her mouth and tries to catch her breath.*)

GUARDED: (*Laughs. Looks back the way they came.*) Wow we ran far. What was that restaurant everyone was headed to?
        (*Silenced gives him a look, points to the duct tape covering her mouth.*)
Right sorry. I think it started with a J, or a G. You don't happen to know sign language do you? Maybe spell it out for me...

SILENCED: (*Hesitates, and then takes off duct tape.*) Giuliano's. (*Puts duct tape back on.*)

GUARDED: Oh right. Thanks. (*Realizes with a panic that his mask is still off. Puts it back on.*) Guess we'll just head back to main street—
        (*Guarded starts to go in one direction, but Silenced grabs*

the back of his shirt and drags him in the opposite direction.)
—Which is that way.

(*They exit offstage.*)

Act I, Scene 4

(*Grief and Dependence come back onstage to the front of the group therapy building. Dependence has success- -fully handcuffed herself to Grief.*)

DEPENDENCE: (*Indicates to the handcuffs, very pleased with herself.*) Told you I'm persistent. (*Does a little celebratory dance.*)

GRIEF: I hate to interrupt your victory dance but... (*Motions to the cuffs.*) Dependence?

DEPENDENCE: What? You don't like the idea of being cuffed to me for all eternity?

GRIEF: You've had your fun. Now unlock me please. Caitlin and I have to get to our friend's art exhibit tonight.

DEPENDENCE: Oh yeah, sorry. I'll have you out in a second.

(*Dependence starts rummaging through her pockets as Grief sets up Caitlin's chair onstage. Suddenly Depend- -ence gets a terrified look on her face and starts going through her pockets all over again.*)

GRIEF: Everything okay?

DEPENDENCE: (*Takes off one of her shoes and shakes it out before putting it back on.*) Yep everything's completely wonderful, normal, and under control.

GRIEF: Dependence...

DEPENDENCE: You haven't seen a key, have you?

GRIEF: You lost the key?!

DEPENDENCE: It—it must've jumped out of my pocket. Keys do that sometimes.

GRIEF: (*Sarcastically.*) Right, as opposed to growing legs and walking away?

DEPENDENCE: Well that would've been my second guess.

GRIEF: It must've fallen out back in the building. Come on.

> (*Grief leaves Caitlin's chair where he set it up onstage. Grief and Dependence walk back to the front door. Dependence tries the door, but it won't open. They exchange a look and Grief also tries the door. It won't budge.*)

DEPENDENCE: Dr. Adams must've locked it.

GRIEF: You gotta be kidding me.

DEPENDENCE: (*Steps back and eyes the door.*) Maybe it's just stuck.

GRIEF: What are you—?
> (*Dependence runs and throws her body against the door, taking Grief with her.*)
Ow! Hey!
> (*Dependence pulls back to ram the door again. Grief blocks the door with his body.*)
No wait stop! Hang on. Do you have Dr. Adams' number?

DEPENDENCE: (*Stops trying to break down the door.*) No, Dr. Adams won't give out her/his number. She/he doesn't want us calling at three a.m. for dating advice.

GRIEF: Yeah, I could see that happening.

DEPENDENCE: Do you know anyone else who could open the door for us?

GRIEF: No.

DEPENDENCE: (*Takes out her phone with her free hand.*) We could call a locksmith.

GRIEF: For the handcuffs or the door?

DEPENDENCE: Either. I bet they could open at least one of them.

GRIEF: (*Takes out his phone with his free hand.*) Okay. Yeah, I'm sure there's one in the area.
(*Both stare at their phones for a couple seconds, and then hold them high up in the air at the same time. Beat. They turn to each other and notice what the other is doing.*)
Oh no.

DEPENDENCE: Ugh! I swear this is the one place in the entire city where you can't get reception. Just last week I was on my phone trying to get concert tickets and... (*Forgets she's handcuffed to Grief and yanks him in the direction she's going.*) Oops, sorry, I forgot.

GRIEF: Okay phones are out. So we'll drive somewhere for help. Where's your car parked?

DEPENDENCE: My car?

GRIEF: Didn't you drive here?

DEPENDENCE: No, I carpooled with my roommate Heartache and she has the keys right now. Did you drive here?

GRIEF: No. My car's in the shop so a friend dropped me and Caitlin off. Another friend is picking us up later for the art exhibit.

DEPENDENCE: Oh no. I'm really sorry Grief. This is not what I thought would happen.

GRIEF: (*Sighs.*) Me neither. This is what I get for never sitting next to you in group therapy.

DEPENDENCE: I'll figure something out. I promise.

(*Grief leans down and picks up Caitlin's chair. In doing so, he has a sudden epiphany.*)

GRIEF: Wait! Wait! I just remembered; I think I saw you put the key in your coat pocket during the session.

DEPENDENCE: Oh right! I left it over there. (*Rushes over to the bench and looks frantically for her jacket, taking Grief along with her.*) It's not here. No. My jacket's gone!

GRIEF: Don't tell me. It grew legs and walked away too.

DEPENDENCE: I swear I left it right there. Someone must've taken it.

GRIEF: Great, so anyone could have it right now.

DEPENDENCE: No, I'm sure Heartache took it. She must've grabbed it knowing we'd drive home together.

GRIEF: Do you know where she went?

DEPENDENCE: I remember she was talking about going to that restaurant she liked. Let's just go there. (*Starts heading offstage, pulling Grief with her.*)

GRIEF: (*Pulls back in resistance.*) I don't think a restaurant is the best place to wear handcuffs.

DEPENDENCE: Oh come on, it'll be fun. We could say that this was a sex experiment gone wrong or that I'm an undercover cop who just arrested you for drug possession.

GRIEF: Look, if the others at the restaurant see us then we'll have to talk about this at the next session...

DEPENDENCE: And if we do I'll do all the talking for you. They'll know it was my fault and you were just an innocent victim. Come on.

GRIEF: (*Sits on the ground in protest.*) No way. This is humiliating enough.

DEPENDENCE: (*Tries to drag him along with her.*) Grief come on, it'll take us forever to get there.

GRIEF: Good! (*Indicates to Caitlin's chair, which he is holding.*) You want to get there sooner then you'll have to carry us.

Act I, Scene 5

(*Unrequited Love and Lost are sitting at the restaurant bar on bar stools. Simon is parked alongside them in his wagon, amusing himself with a Rubik's cube or flipping through an adult magazine. A bartender is serving Lost and Unrequited Love drinks.*)

BARTENDER: (*Hands drink to Unrequited Love.*) Jameson on the rocks for the lady. (*Hands drink to Lost.*) Gin and Tonic for the gentleman. (*Hands a very large drink to Simon.*) And an extra-large Cosmopolitan for the baggage.

(*Bartender exits before Lost or Unrequited Love can respond.*)

UNREQUITED LOVE: (*Stirs her drink. Clears throat.*) So, what do you do for a living?

LOST: I'm a biomedical engineer.

UNREQUITED LOVE: I'm gonna pretend I know what that means.

LOST: Um, it just means that I design artificial hearts and pacemakers for people.

UNREQUITED LOVE: Oh. So you save lives.

LOST: Not really. I just design stuff.

(*They each take a sip of their drinks. Lost laughs slightly.*)

UNREQUITED LOVE: What's so funny?

LOST: Nothing, it's just...when I talk to girls there's always this intense awkwardness. But that's not happening here.

UNREQUITED LOVE: (*Teasingly.*) Uh oh, now you've jinxed it.

LOST: (*Laughs nervously.*) Sorry. Um...so, do you think you'll find someone for a second date soon?

UNREQUITED LOVE: I may have found someone but...
 (*Simon burps. Loudly. Unrequited Love indicates to Simon.*)
I have some baggage I guess.

LOST: Well, at least yours is obvious. I mean with most people it takes a few months for them to show any signs of craziness but you just have it right there in front for all to see and they know going in that you're...
 (*Unrequited Love looks at him. He clears his throat.*)
So, do you like this someone?

UNREQUITED LOVE: Yeah. I think so. We work at the same design company. He's even come close to asking me out a couple times, but for some reason didn't. (*Looks at Simon.*) Maybe he thinks I'm too conspicuous.

LOST: What do you like about him?

UNREQUITED LOVE: His heart.

LOST: I mean on the outside, like personality-wise. Something you can see.

UNREQUITED LOVE: But I do see. It's easy to see love in

a person's heart.

    (*Beat. Lost looks confused.*)

What? Can't you see it?

LOST: Love? No not really. I have trouble understanding that word or anything associated with it.

UNREQUITED LOVE: Oh.

    (*Simon snaps his fingers. Unrequited Love and Lost immediately freeze onstage.*)

SIMON: (*Speaks in an aside to the audience.*) Sorry I know I'm not supposed to interrupt, but I just need a break. And by break, I mean a drink. (*Takes a sip from his glass and stretches out. He can get up and strut about the stage.*) Honestly, I wasn't trained as a professional model or anything and sitting still for so long is no piece of cake. I mean, I guess I'm okay with being towed around all day and all night. It's only for one day of the week. And Mondays are never fun to be at work anyway, so I guess I shouldn't be complaining, but I do miss my girlfriend. We just moved in together you know? And she doesn't exactly understand the whole need to be gone on Mondays to exist as a metaphorical symbol of past pining for an old acquaintance. Man, this is good. (*Successfully drains his entire drink.*) I hope they serve these during intermission.

    (*Simon holds his empty drink up and snaps his fingers. The other characters unfreeze. Bartender reappears.*)

BARTENDER: Refill?

UNREQUITED LOVE: (*Looks at her and Lost's full glasses.*) Oh no thank you I think we're...

BARTENDER: (*Indicates towards Simon, who is holding up his giant empty glass.*) Girly drink number two. (*Refills Simon's drink, exits.*)

LOST: (*Indicates to Unrequited Love's coat, which she still has on.*) Aren't you warm?

UNREQUITED LOVE: Nope, I'm good. (*Indicates to Lost's coat, which he still has on.*) Are you warm?

LOST: Not yet.

UNREQUITED LOVE: So...do you have anyone in mind for a second date? Or even a first date I guess...

LOST: Not at the moment. But even if I did, flirting isn't really my strong suit.

UNREQUITED LOVE: Well, then we must remedy that. (*Picks up her drink to take a sip.*) Okay, pretend I'm a single female sitting next to you at a bar.

LOST: Well, technically you are a single female sitting next to me at a bar...

UNREQUITED LOVE: Look, you see me, a lonely girl having a drink. What do you do?

LOST: Avoid eye contact at all costs?

UNREQUITED LOVE: Oh come on, don't you ever randomly flirt and find yourself falling in love with attractive young women?

LOST: I've forgotten how.

UNREQUITED LOVE: How peculiar.

LOST: (*Struggles, trying to find the right words.*) No...I mean I did once, but I've forgotten most things about love I guess. It just comes with the territory of losing your heart.

UNREQUITED LOVE: Wait. (*Beat.*) You lost your heart?

LOST: Yeah um...I lost my heart about a year ago. Filed a police report and everything, but they haven't had any luck finding it.

UNREQUITED LOVE: But without a heart, how can you—

LOST: Love? I can't.

UNREQUITED LOVE: Can you remember what love feels like?

LOST: (*Shrugs.*) Vaguely, but for the most part I don't remember much about it. Like when couples hold hands, I don't understand why they do that.

UNREQUITED LOVE: Must make for some lonely nights.

(*They sit and swirl their drinks without taking sips. Simon leans forward and snaps his fingers. Lost and Unrequited Love freeze.*)

SIMON: (*Addresses the audience. Still has the option of getting up out of the wagon and strutting about the stage.*) And another thing...I don't mind the wagon that much, but I just wish it was a little bigger you know? I don't know if you can see from the back row, but there's not a lot of legroom here. I mean why can't she put in a bar or a bidet or something? And is it just me, or does our bartender sound a lot like Dr. Adams? Almost like we couldn't afford another actor to play the role. (*Relieved sigh.*) Wow that felt good to get off my chest. I should do this more often. Man, I'm going to need another refill soon. (*Manages to drain his whole glass.*) Okay, I'm good. I'm good. Now back to the show. Oh, and don't do drugs.

(*Simon snaps his fingers. The other characters onstage unfreeze. As if on cue, the Bartender reappears again.*)

BARTENDER: Another refill for the hard-drinking metaphor.

(*They all look to Simon, who is holding up his large empty glass again. Bartender refills his drink and exits.*)

UNREQUITED LOVE: Do you miss it? Your heart?

LOST: Every day. I had trouble dating before I lost it. Now it just makes it worse.

UNREQUITED LOVE: So where'd you lose it?

LOST: (*Not the best liar.*) I don't know.

UNREQUITED LOVE: How bout when?

LOST: I'd rather not talk about it.

UNREQUITED LOVE: You're not gonna get any closer to

finding your heart until you figure out the who, what, when, where, and why.

LOST: (*Softly.*) December twenty-third.

UNREQUITED LOVE: What?

LOST: December twenty-third. My girlfriend...she broke up with me in a text message while I was driving. When I saw the text, I lost control and crashed into a tree. I remember waking up in the hospital and feeling this emptiness inside of me, and then I realized that I'd lost my heart in the accident. (*Realizes he's probably said too much.*) Sorry, I didn't mean to pile all that on you like that. We do enough to each other in group therapy. I can just hear Dr. Adams ask, "And how do you feel about that Lost?"

UNREQUITED LOVE: (*Sarcastically.*) And how DO you feel about that Lost?

LOST: (*Laughs.*) To be honest, it actually feels good to confide in someone.

UNREQUITED LOVE: So, tell me. Where is this tree? They always say look in the last place first.

LOST: Look for what?

UNREQUITED LOVE: Your heart...where did you say the accident was?

LOST: Oh, on some residential street near her house. It's actually about a twenty-minute drive from here.

(*Unrequited Love stands up, grabbing her things.*)
Are you leaving?

UNREQUITED LOVE: Yeah. If we're going to find your heart we'd better get going.

LOST: (*Shocked.*) What? You really want to help me find...?

UNREQUITED LOVE: Yes of course. Let's go.

(*The Bartender enters and starts to clean up the bar. Lost takes out money from his wallet and leaves it on the bar counter to pay for the drinks. Simon, on the other hand, flings monopoly money into the air, making it rain.*)

BARTENDER: (*Picks up the monopoly money.*) Mondays...

(*Unrequited Love pulls the wagon away from the bar while Lost pushes it from behind. They exit offstage.*)

Act I, Scene 6

(*Heartache approaches Desire, who is sitting at the rest-*
-aurant bar. A liquor bottle sits on the counter next to him.
He is drinking from a shot glass.)

HEARTACHE: They said a table would be ready soon. Also I think I just saw Lost and Unrequited Love drive away together. I wonder where— (*Notices that he is drinking.*) Desire, what are you doing?

DESIRE: (*Throws back a shot before answering her.*) I'm drowning my sorrows.

HEARTACHE: Looks more like your sorrows are drowning you.

DESIRE: Yeah well, there's only so much that group therapy can help you with.

HEARTACHE: (*Grabs the liquor bottle and clinks it with his glass.*) I'll join you in that regard. (*Drinks straight from the liquor bottle and looks around the restaurant.*) Lots of couples here tonight.

DESIRE: Oh...hadn't noticed.

HEARTACHE: A lot of them are dancing.

DESIRE: Didn't notice that either.

HEARTACHE: (*Looks out a window.*) It sure got dark outside quickly... (*Indicates to Desire's glasses.*) So you wear those at night too?

DESIRE: Yeah.

HEARTACHE: Are you trying to set a fashion statement?

DESIRE: Sure. Why not?

HEARTACHE: Good luck getting people to wear dark lenses day and night.

DESIRE: Why? I don't see much difference between the two.

HEARTACHE: Wow, you might be even more pessimistic than I am. (*Tilts her head to listen to a song that is being played over the restaurant loudspeakers.*) Oh, they're playing that song, that new song that just came out.
    (*Desire looks at her blankly and just shrugs his shoulders. He doesn't know the song.*)
Come on. (*Stands up with her cane and grabs Desire's hand, trying to pull him towards the dance floor.*) Why don't you take a dance with me to forget your troubles? You said so yourself that endorphins are good for the body.

DESIRE: No thanks. I don't dance.

HEARTACHE: We'd basically just be swaying. Or we could just do a couple steps like this. (*Leans on her cane and does a couple of dance steps.*) See?

DESIRE: No I don't see. Uh, I mean I'm just tired from the walk. I'd rather sit here. Thanks though.

HEARTACHE: (*Sighs. Sits next to him. The song fades out.*) It's just as well. Dancing is too romantic sometimes.

DESIRE: So you're not a rom-com person.

HEARTACHE: No, I don't do romance. One-night stands are more my thing. If we weren't in therapy together I would've definitely hooked up with you by now.

DESIRE: Um, going back to the first part of that statement...What's wrong with romance?

HEARTACHE: (*Throws up her hands in frustration.*) Oh my God, so much—

DESIRE: (*Rests his chin on his fist in a mocking intellectual pose.*) Oh do tell.

HEARTACHE: Romance leads to relationships. Relation--ships lead to betrayal. And betrayal leads to pain...and I can't bear pain. (*Reaches into her purse for a medicine bottle. She takes a couple pills out and pops them into her mouth, then takes a sip from the liquor bottle to wash it all down.*) Yeah. So no romance.

DESIRE: (*Reaches out for the medicine bottle, takes it, and feels it with his hands. Shakes it near his ear.*) What do you take these for?

HEARTACHE: Heart problems.

DESIRE: You sure it's safe to mix alcohol with them?

HEARTACHE: I've done it before. It makes no difference.

DESIRE: You probably shouldn't...

HEARTACHE: Yeah and you shouldn't drink so much, so don't judge.

DESIRE: Okay fine.

HEARTACHE: Fine.

DESIRE: (*Looks down at the empty shot glass in his hands. Sighs and pushes it away.*) If you're not looking for anything serious, then why even come to the sessions? I thought the whole concept of hooking up was intimacy with no strings attached.

HEARTACHE: I only come because my roommate Dependence drags me to it every week against my will. And let me tell you that driving while handcuffed is no joy ride.

DESIRE: Oooooh, that makes sense. She must be interesting to live with.

HEARTACHE: Interesting being the code word for complicated. But she's actually pretty fun to live with. She's entertaining. Especially when she brings home guys. Most of them end up with me by the end of the night.

DESIRE: Okay then.

> (*Grief and Dependence burst into the room. Dependence is carrying Grief on her back. Grief is holding onto Caitlin's chair.*)

DEPENDENCE: There they are! (*Drops Grief to the floor, dragging him along with her.*)

GRIEF: (*Struggles to stand and keep up with Dependence as they approach Heartache and Desire.*) Ow! Watch it!

(*Heartache looks up in alarm at the two of them. Desire turns toward them.*)

DEPENDENCE: Heartache! Desire! I'm so glad you're here.

HEARTACHE: What happened?

GRIEF: Not important.

DEPENDENCE: Heartache, I need to borrow the car.

HEARTACHE: It's my car. And no way.

DEPENDENCE & GRIEF: What?

HEARTACHE: The last time you drove it while handcuffed you rear-ended an old lady at a stoplight.

DEPENDENCE: Oh yeah. She wasn't happy...

GRIEF: I'm sure we can manage—

HEARTACHE: Yes, you both seem to have everything under control. I can't imagine why everyone's staring.

DEPENDENCE: Heartache, I'm begging you—

HEARTACHE: And you'll be thanking me when you see that I'm saving your life. Just call a locksmith and order a meal or something while you wait.

GRIEF: Fine. We'll ask for a table then.

HOST: (*From offstage.*) Table for Heartache?

HEARTACHE: (*Eager to be rid of Dependence.*) Look, just take our table, okay? I want to finish my drink in peace.

(*Grief drags Dependence away with him.*)

DEPENDENCE: Don't mind Heartache. She's just pissed that I dragged her to therapy again. She'll get over it in a day or two.

GRIEF: Hopefully it won't take the locksmith that long to get here.

(*They exit.*)

Act I, Scene 7

(*At the restaurant, Grief and Dependence are sitting at a table together. Their handcuffed hands rest on the table in front of them. Grief has Caitlin's chair set up beside him. A waiter approaches them.*)

WAITER: (*Places two drinks in front of Grief and Dependence.*) Two lemonades for the officer and her detainee, enjoy. (*Exits.*)

GRIEF: I can't believe we're doing this. In public.

DEPENDENCE: The locksmith said she'd call me when she's close by.

GRIEF: That's good. My friend said he'd be here in about forty minutes to pick me and Caitlin up for the show. I'd rather not have to explain this to him.

DEPENDENCE: I've said I was sorry like five—

GRIEF: —Seven.

DEPENDENCE: Seven times. I don't know what else to say to make you forgive me.

GRIEF: No worries. I'll let you know when I think of it.

DEPENDENCE: So...Heartache and Desire together at the bar...you and me...

GRIEF: Yeah, it's funny how we've all paired off into groups.

Like none of us can stand being without human companionship. (*Attempts to take a sip of his drink.*)

DEPENDENCE: Come on. Life is more fun when you have someone to share it with. (*Raises her glass, but in doing so causes Grief to spit his drink out.*)

GRIEF: (*Coughs.*) Provided you're not handcuffed to them while trying to drink.

DEPENDENCE: Oops. Sorry. So, you said you're going to an art exhibit? It sounds like you're serious about putting yourself back out there.

GRIEF: (*Trying to dry himself.*) Getting back into the social mix is easy. The dating area is a bit trickier.

DEPENDENCE: You're a good-looking guy. You shouldn't have any trouble finding a Friday night date.

GRIEF: No, I always struggle with meeting new people these days.

DEPENDENCE: People? Or people of a certain gender?

GRIEF: Okay, women. It's hard to meet women. Caitlin is always with me and I have to balance the date between the two women.

DEPENDECE: So your dates don't like having Caitlin around?

GRIEF: Most of them are polite about it. But other times I

feel like there's no way I can make a date work with two women in my life.

DEPENDENCE: Well you seem to be making it work now. I don't mind Caitlin's company, and she seems perfectly content with me, although it has been a disruptive evening so far—

GRIEF: Wait a minute, are you counting this as a date?

DEPENDENCE: I'd say it could pass as one to the random bystander.

GRIEF: Then this has been one of the more adventurous dates I've been on.

DEPENDENCE: And we didn't even have to go mini golfing.

GRIEF: You know...it would make sense that you and she would get along...

DEPENDENCE: Who? Caitlin? Why?

GRIEF: Well it's just...you're both strong people.

DEPENDENCE: (*Raises her hand to highlight the fact that they're still handcuffed together.*) Yes, because a girl who clings to others is definitely strong.

GRIEF: I don't mean that, I mean you're strong in yourself like, you know who you are and don't try to convince yourself otherwise.

DEPENDENCE: Don't give me too much credit. I'm still handcuffed to you...you know.

GRIEF: Yes, I'm quite aware of that. But I kinda like it. It's nice to feel needed. Usually after these group sessions I just head home alone and watch whatever random shows are on TV.

DEPENDENCE: But you're not alone. You have Caitlin.

GRIEF: Yeah I do, but lately she's become a bit...distant.

DEPENDENCE: But you saw that movie with her yesterday. Wasn't that fun?

GRIEF: Yes, but she was antsy the whole time, like she wanted to leave.

DEPENDENCE: But she didn't.

GRIEF: No. I asked her to stay.

DEPENDENCE: You didn't let her go?

GRIEF: I told her she could leave if she wanted, but that I really wanted her to stay.

DEPENDENCE: Has she always been with you since, you know?

GRIEF: Yeah. A few days before her funeral, Caitlin told me that she'd look after me even when she left. That I wouldn't have to worry about coming home to an empty house because she'd be there.

DEPENDENCE: And she was?

GRIEF: Yep, and she's been with me every day since.

DEPENDENCE: Sounds like she cares about you very much.

GRIEF: Yes, but things are changing. I've started working at a new restaurant and have different hours than she's used to. I've been thinking about moving closer to work...

DEPENDENCE: Oh.

GRIEF: And I got a cat. (*Beat.*) She hates cats.

DEPENDENCE: Oh. That was a bold move.

GRIEF: With each change I make, she seems more distant. Like she's already packed her suitcase and is staying just to humor me. One day I'm afraid I'll wake up and she'll be gone.

DEPENDENCE: I'm sure you're just imagining that.

GRIEF: I hope so. (*Dependence suddenly looks around the restaurant.*) What are you looking for?

DEPENDENCE: The restroom.

GRIEF: Oh mother of—Can't you wait?

DEPENDENCE: Nope. Come on. (*Gets up.*)

GRIEF: (*Resists her attempt to get him out of his seat.*) Oh no. No thank you. You've tortured me enough. I'm way too far outside my comfort zone already.

DEPENDENCE: Then you can go outside it just a little bit

more. Please it'll be quick and this dress is brand new. (*Beat.*) Please?

GRIEF: (*Beat. Grief makes a face.*) Okay.
    (*Dependence starts to drag him offstage. Grief suddenly turns back in a panic.*)
Wait! I need Caitlin.

DEPENDENCE: No time! Come on!

GRIEF: Wait, no! (*Looks back at Caitlin's chair in alarm as Dependence drags him offstage.*)

Act I, Scene 8

(Guarded and Silenced are standing together at the restaurant's entrance. Guarded is talking to one of the restaurant hosts.)

HOST: Can I get your name?

GUARDED: Guarded.

HOST: Say again?

GUARDED: *(Hesitates. Takes off his mask.)* Guarded.
(Host looks down, making a note of Guarded's name.)
Uh, could we have a table for two please?

HOST: Well, we don't have any seats available right now. Dinner rush just started. *(Looks up at Guarded, taking in his appearance.)* You escape from quarantine or something?

GUARDED: What? Oh, no not really.

HOST: Thought I'd ask, you never know when a new plague might start. So I can actually squeeze you in if you're willing to wait a bit. Or you could just sit at the bar?

GUARDED: *(Looks at Silenced, who shakes her head slightly.)* Um, I think we're okay with waiting, thanks. *(Puts his mask back on.)*

HOST: Okay, just stay nearby in case your name gets called.

(Guarded and Silenced both go to a bench outside the restaurant. Guarded circles the bench, trying to find a

clean spot. Silenced sits. Guarded finally brushes off a spot and sits. There's an awkward silence.)

GUARDED: So...do you take bribes to talk? (*Silenced shakes her head.*) We could always discuss the weather. That's a safe topic.

> (*Silenced shrugs. Guarded looks down, noticing that the rug on the ground is crooked. He leans forward and fixes it. Not satisfied, he leans forward and fixes it again. He even takes out a comb to straighten the threads on the side.*)

SILENCED: (*Peels off her duct tape, annoyed by his OCD.*) Your life's legacy isn't going to be whether or not that rug is straight. (*Puts the duct tape back on.*)
> (*Guarded looks up, acknowledging her words, but continues to fix the rug. Finally, he gets up and tries to fix the rug from a different angle. Then sits. As he leans forward again, Silenced puts her foot on the rug to stop him, taking off her duct tape. Fixes Guarded with a stare.*)
Move it again...I dare you.

GUARDED: (*Stops fixing the rug.*) No I'm good.

SILENCED: (*Indicates to Guarded's medical mask and medical gloves.*) Okay...I gotta ask, are you in the medical field or did you actually escape from quarantine?

GUARDED: Neither. These are just precautions.

SILENCED: For?

GUARDED: Uh...it's complicated...

SILENCED: Don't...people just say that when they don't want to explain further? (*Moves to put the duct tape back on.*)

GUARDED: Wait! Why don't you talk more at our sessions? The others might like what you have to say.

SILENCED: But I wouldn't know what to say and my face would get all hot and red like it always does.

GUARDED: Well, I'm sure all those times you haven't said anything, you've certainly thought of a lot to say. It might mix things up a bit.

SILENCED: (*Shakes her head*) I—I don't have that much to say. (*Hurriedly puts duct tape over mouth.*)

GUARDED: But it's the quiet ones that have the most to say. The talkative ones don't say anything.
(*Silenced suddenly acts like she's going to sneeze.*)
Might be easier if you take off the—

SILENCED: (*Rips off her duct tape and places it on the bench between her and Guarded.*) Achoo! Achoo! Achoo!

GUARDED: (*Grabs the piece of duct tape and hides it in his pocket.*) Bless you.

SILENCED: Thank you— (*Looks for the duct tape, then panics and searches desperately for it.*)

GUARDED: Wouldn't you know it? While you were sneezing, a bird snatched up the tape and just flew away.
(*Silenced gives him a look and holds her hand out to him expectantly.*)

Don't look at me; it was a pretty tough-looking bird. Not something you'd mess with.
(*Silenced lets her hand fall into her lap in annoyance. She puts a hand over her mouth.*)
Oh come on. You don't need to cover your mouth. It's not like your silence is contagious. Why can't you talk to me?

SILENCED: (*Uncovers her mouth.*) But you're not sick either and you wear that mask. I bet you couldn't go a minute without it on.

GUARDED: Hey I actually have a good reason for this precaution. Do you have any idea how many germs are floating in the air right now?

SILENCED: No but as I'm sure you brought up that question just so you could answer it yourself pleeeeaaaase do so. (*Covers her mouth.*)

GUARDED: For someone who never talks in our group sessions you sure have a lot to say now.

SILENCED: (*Uncovers her mouth.*) You're just trying to make me angry so I'll talk.

GUARDED: Well it's working isn't it?

SILENCED: Ugh stop! (*Fans her face rapidly.*) You're making me blush. I hate when I blush.

GUARDED: You shouldn't. I think it's endearing.

SILENCED: Whatever that means... (*Takes her wallet out of her purse and waves it at Guarded temptingly.*) Come on. I'll bet all the money in my wallet that you can't survive a full minute breathing the same, infected air as everybody else.

GUARDED: (*Stands up, takes off his mask. Holds it in his hands.*) Fine. There, you see?

SILENCED: (*Stands.*) And how do you feel?

GUARDED: Wonderful.

SILENCED: Really? You don't feel the slightest bit nauseous? Maybe a little dizzy?

GUARDED: Ha-ha, nope.

SILENCED: (*Walks towards him.*) Not even if I was to stand a little bit closer?

GUARDED: (*Voice cracks.*) Not even then.

SILENCED: Huh. You're not holding your breath are you?

GUARDED: (*Shakes his head with his mouth firmly closed.*) Mhm. Mhm.

SILENCED: (*Leans forward and closes Guarded's nose with her fingers.*) How bout now?

> (*Guarded slowly takes out a can of air disinfectant from his pocket. Suddenly he pushes Silenced away and frant--ically sprays the air around him.*)

GUARDED: Sorry. I panicked. (*Sprays the can of air disinfectant once more in Silenced's direction.*)

SILENCED: (*Coughs and fans the air in front of her.*) God, I bet hooking up is impossible with that mask on.

GUARDED: No comment. (*Moves to put mask back on.*)

SILENCED: (*Grabs the mask from Guarded's hands before he can put it back on.*) Honestly how do you kiss girls with this thing? Or is it a turn on to them? I guess you could play the whole doctor patient sex angle but at some point I'm guessing the mask has to come off...among other things...

GUARDED: (*Covers his ears.*) Stop. Stop. Stop.

SILENCED: Sorry, maybe that's not something I want to know after all. (*Beat. Guarded tries to grab his mask back. Silenced moves away.*) Seriously how do you kiss?

GUARDED: I don't.

SILENCED: So you've never kissed anyone.

GUARDED: I have. But it was awkward and stuff. (*Shakes his head, suddenly desperate to change the subject.*) And besides, kissing is so dangerous when you think about it.

SILENCED: Really?

GUARDED: Come on Silenced, kissing is the quickest way to get sick.

SILENCED: And what exactly are you so afraid of catching? Chicken pox? Herpes?

GUARDED: Love.

SILENCED: Aw....

GUARDED: No. No. It's not cute. It's a cruel sickness that takes no mercy on its victims. Trust me, love isn't worth the pain it causes. You're the lucky one, you'll never know what it's like to be kissed or have a relationship—

SILENCED: (*In a warning tone.*) Wait, I'm sorry, you think I've never been kissed or had a real relationship?

GUARDED: (*Doesn't catch her warning tone, unaware that he's offended her.*) Well yeah, I mean it's kinda obvious. You clearly don't want to get involved with anyone or you wouldn't wear that tape all the time. But that's a good thing. I mean, the fact that you keep everyone at bay so you'll never have to deal with an actual relationship is—

SILENCED: (*Gives Guarded a look.*) —Stop. You don't know anything about me, okay?

GUARDED: (*Realizes too late that he's said the wrong thing.*) You're right, I don't. I'm sorry.

(*Beat.*)

SILENCED: Can I have my tape back?

GUARDED: Can I have my mask back?

SILENCED: (*Hands Guarded his mask back.*) Fine. Here.

(*Guarded gives Silenced her tape back, but it's twisted and unusable. Silenced begins to walk offstage.*)

GUARDED: Wait, where are you going?

SILENCED: I need something to drink.

GUARDED: I'm coming with you. (*Puts his mask back on.*)

SILENCED: Okay, but don't expect me to talk to you.

(*Guarded and Silenced exit the stage together.*)

Act I, Scene 9

(*Dependence and Grief emerge from offstage and return to their table at the restaurant.*)

GRIEF: Well, I certainly have never done that before.

DEPENDENCE: First time for everything.

GRIEF: I always did wonder what the inside of a women's restroom looked like.
(*Dependence shoots him a sideways glance, perplexed.*)
No, no, not like that...I mean like if there was a secret room or bar or something that never got installed in our bathroom. It would've made sense for all those packs of girls that go in together.

DEPENDENCE: Oh yeah, there's a secret room. You just have to press a button under the sink for it.

GRIEF: Huh...Okay, so now I guess we wait—

(*Grief stops dead when he sees that Caitlin's chair has disappeared from the stage. There is a note on the floor where the audience last saw Caitlin's chair. Grief picks up the note and reads it.*)

DEPENDENCE: Grief? What's wrong?

GRIEF: She's gone.

DEPENDENCE: What?

GRIEF: Caitlin's gone.

DPENDENCE: (*Looks around the restaurant in confusion.*) What? Where?

GRIEF: I leave her without warning and she must've panicked. Why did I leave her alone?

DEPENDENCE: Does her note say where she's gone?

GRIEF: What do you care? This is your fault. You just couldn't resist handcuffing yourself to me and now she's gone. My wife is gone.

DEPENDENCE: Yes you mentioned that.

GRIEF: Oh you're no help.

DEPENDENCE: Grief no, I'm sorry. I didn't think—

GRIEF: You don't think, you don't think. Do you ever think about anyone but yourself?

DEPENDENCE: I do! Let me help you find her. She couldn't have gone far.

GRIEF: I don't need any help from you.

DEPENDECE: Please Grief. If I only do one thing right tonight it'll be finding Caitlin.

GRIEF: No. I'm done with you. I can't even look at you right now. (*Turns away from Dependence and walks in the opposite direction, taking her with him.*)

DEPENDENCE: Then wait for the locksmith to separate us and I'll leave you alone.

GRIEF: I don't have time to wait for her. I have to find Caitlin now!

DEPENDENCE: Grief, calm down. This isn't going to help Caitlin. What did the note say?

GRIEF: (*Shoves the note into Dependence's hands.*) Here.

DEPENDENCE: (*Reads the note.*) "Went to get some air. Love Caitlin." Well that helps. She could get air anywhere.

GRIEF: Not really. You don't know Caitlin like I do.

DEPENDENCE: Then tell me what I need to know to help. I'm guessing this has never happened before so—

GRIEF: (*Sighs.*) No, this is the twelfth time she's disappeared.

DEPENDENCE: What?

GRIEF: She's left me before, but usually her note says exactly where she's gone. I just have to go to one of our old haunts. Like the restaurant where we had our first date or the hiking trail we'd always take on Saturday mornings. Once I find her, then she always comes back with me.

DEPENDENCE: So, this is normal.

GRIEF: (*Takes the note back.*) More of a new normal...but her note's never been this vague before. And she always leaves when we're at home, never in a public setting like this. I need to find her. (*Folds the note and sticks it in his pocket.*)

DEPENDENCE: Maybe we can get some help from them. (*Goes over to where Heartache and Desire are sitting, dragging Grief with her.*) Hey. Desperate emergency. Caitlin's gone missing. We need to find her.

GRIEF: Look I'm sorry. I hate to ask either of you to sacrifice your night for this.

HEARTACHE: (*Twirls her finger at their handcuffed hands.*) Only if you promise to share how this whole thing happened at our next session.

GRIEF: Fine.

HEARTACHE: Then of course, what can I do?

DESIRE: I'll help too.

HEARTACHE: You don't have to.

DESIRE: I want to.

GRIEF: I think we should split up. Caitlin usually goes to only a few specific places. I'll text you the addresses of a couple of them to check out, and we'll cover the rest.

DEPENDENCE: And you expect us to walk there?

HEARTACHE: (*Reaches into her purse and takes out her car keys.*) Fine. I'll make an exception for Caitlin. Take the car.

It's parked back at the therapy building. But if you crash it you're paying for it. We'll take Desire's car.

DESIRE: (*Reaches out to try and stop her.*) Wait Heartache no—

DEPENDENCE: (*Grabs the car keys.*) Thanks roomie! (*Grabs Grief.*) Come on Grief! We're burning moonlight! (*Starts to run offstage.*)

GRIEF: (*Calls back over his shoulder.*) Thanks, I owe you one.

(*Dependence and Grief exit the stage.*)

HEARTACHE: (*Uses her cane to hoist herself up. Starts to walk out of the restaurant.*) Let's start walking. I'm guessing you're parked back at the therapy building too.

DESIRE: (*Follows behind her slowly.*) No, I mean...

HEARTACHE: Where then?

DESIRE: Heartache I can't...

HEARTACHE: What?

DESIRE: I can't drive.

HEARTACHE: (*Walks out of the restaurant with Desire walking carefully beside her.*) Relax, you only had a couple shots, and with your body weight that's not enough to make you unfit to drive.

DESIRE: (*Reaches out and takes her arm, stopping her.*) Heartache no—

HEARTACHE: Fine. It if it makes you feel better I'll drive.

DESIRE: Heartache I didn't drive here. I don't drive.

HEARTACHE: Oh, I guess I just assumed you drove here. Did you never learn how?

DESIRE: No I learned. It's just not feasible right now.

HEARTACHE: So you're protesting gas prices aaaand making a fashion statement? (*Points to his glasses.*)

DESIRE: No I just don't drive.

HEARTACHE: Ooookay, then how'd you get here?

DESIRE: A...um...family member dropped me off.

HEARTACHE: (*Takes out her phone.*) Ugh...Let's just get an Uber then. (*Sees the unoccupied bench outside the restaurant. She takes Desire's arm and draws him towards it.*) We can wait here.

DESIRE: Okay.

HEARTACHE: (*Looks at her phone, and then at Desire, and then back at her phone.*) So...there's a driver that can be here in twenty minutes.

DESIRE: What? That's way too long.

HEARTACHE: (*Grimaces in pain and puts her hand to her heart.*) Life is full of disappointments. (*Turns away from Desire so that her back is to him, but he is still close to her.*) Now, take for example...

DESIRE: Take what for example?
    (*Heartache starts to teeter.*)
Heartache?
    (*Heartache faints backwards, trust-falling into Desire's arms. She drops her cane as Desire catches her.*)
Heartache. That's not funny. Heartache!

INTERMISSION

Act II, Scene 1

(*Simon walks onstage with an armful of concession stand goodies.*)

SIMON: (*Notices the audience.*) Oh hello, were you expecting someone else? Oh, right you're probably wondering what happened to Heartache. Don't worry, as far as I know she only dies in the Shakespeare version of this play. (*Suddenly realizes that he should explain his appearance.*) Oh, and this? Actors get discounts on intermission concessions. And speaking of concessions, please take this moment to unwrap all annoying snacks and turn off your cell phones. I should warn you that as actors we tend to get violent when we hear ringtones. Took us forever to clean up after that last guy. (*Beat.*) But anyways, how bout we get back to the show and I to my wagon? And with that I bid you good night good night, parting is such sweet sorrow, that I shall say good night till it be...wait we're not doing the Shakespeare version tonight. (*Exits.*)

Act II, Scene 2

(*Unrequited Love and Lost are driving in Unrequited Love's car. Simon is in the backseat, wearing a sleep mask and a neck pillow.*)

LOST: (*Points to the left.*) It's just over there. The ash tree with the dark scratches on it.

(*They park. Unrequited Love turns off the car. The two of them get out and walk towards the tree together.*)

UNREQUITED LOVE: (*Stops and turns back.*) Wait, Simon!

LOST: Oh right, I'll help you get him out.

UNREQUITED LOVE: Thanks, I... (*Stops.*)

LOST: What's up?

UNREQUITED LOVE: You know what, um...
    (*Simon snores.*)
He's asleep. Let's just leave him there for now.

LOST: Alright.

UNREQUITED LOVE: So when was the last time you were here?

LOST: Um...right after I got out of the hospital. I came thinking my heart might still be here.

UNREQUITED LOVE: A logical assumption...

LOST: I searched for an hour. Even brought a ladder and climbed up into the tree. But I couldn't find anything. I never thought I'd come back. Well, until now.

UNREQUITED LOVE: This place must hold some awful memories. (*Realizes that she has stirred up some pain in bringing Lost here.*) I am so sorry I made you come here. Do you want to leave?

LOST: No...not yet. As long as we're here I might as well look again.

UNREQUITED LOVE: (*Takes Lost's hand and pulls him towards the tree.*) Then come on. With two people you'll find it twice as fast.

(*Simon snaps his fingers. Lost and Unrequited Love freeze, facing away from him.*)

SIMON: (*Stretches, takes off his eye mask.*) Aw did I sleep through the whole scene? I hate when I do that. (*Shrugs.*) Eh, whatever. I'll just get someone backstage to tell me what happened. Although the fact that she's holding his hand tells me what I need to know. And if she's with him...Hey! (*Takes out phone and dials number.*) Then I...am not needed here anymore...Hey babe, I'm coming home early tonight. Break out the Christmas lingerie and order a pizza. (*Beat.*) Oh you know I'll wear the Santa hat. Alright, see you soon! (*Hangs up the phone and gets out of the car. Starts to go offstage, but then he turns around and goes to the trunk, where the wagon is.*) Better make sure I don't leave any of my stuff behind. (*Reaches into the wagon and takes out random things, like a teddy bear, a fake flower bouquet, a tennis racket, a coloring book, etc. until he picks up Dependence's jacket.*) Wait this isn't...oh yeah this is from that girl with the handcuffs. Might as well take it with me. Maybe I'll run into her in the next scene. (*Exits.*)

(*Lost and Unrequited Love are left frozen onstage for a couple of seconds. Then Simon comes back onstage quickly.*)

SIMON: Oops! Almost forgot. (*Snaps his fingers and exits.*)

(*Unrequited Love and Lost unfreeze.*)

UNREQUITED LOVE: How bout you take the right side of the tree and I'll take the left side?

LOST: Okay.

UNREQUITED LOVE: I'll meet you in the middle.

Act II, Scene 3

(*In a hospital room. Heartache is lying on the hospital bed, dressed in a hospital gown, asleep. Desire is asleep in a chair next to her bed. Heartache suddenly awakens and sits up in a panic. She looks around the room and sees Desire.*)

HEARTACHE: What happened?

DESIRE: (*Starts and looks in her direction.*) Oh good you're awake.

HEARTACHE: Where am I?

DESIRE: I'd say a hospital, but I wouldn't rule out an insane asylum. They haven't tried to put a straitjacket on you have they?

HEARTACHE: Desire!

DESIRE: Sorry. You're at St. Margaret's Hospital. You had a bad reaction to mixing those pills with alcohol.

HEARTACHE: What? That's ridiculous.

DESIRE: Told you not to mix the two.

HEARTACHE: (*Looks around her in alarm.*) No. No. Forget it. I'm not staying here. I hate hospitals.

DESIRE: I hate them too. But you're not going anywhere.

HEARTACHE: Trust me I'm fine. Where's my purse? Ah,

there it is. My cane, I need my cane. (*Notices that Desire is holding her cane.*) Can you hand me that please?

DESIRE: Heartache, wait. There's another reason they want to keep you here.

HEARTACHE: If they want to harvest my organs that badly they should've tied me down. I'm leaving. I have the right as a patient to resist medical treatment.

DESIRE: Heartache, they want to keep you under observation. They think you took the pills on purpose.

HEARTACHE: I already told you. I take them for my heart. I have a doctor's prescription and everything.

DESIRE: M-hm. And the alcohol...

HEARTACHE: I've mixed the two before and was fine. Why should I have expected tonight to be any different? I'm not the guilty party here. Now give me my cane.

DESIRE: Heartache, you're not listening. They think you meant to do it. Like an intentional overdose.

HEARTACHE: But you were with me. You saw that I only took a couple. It must've been the strong alcohol. Usually I just have wine with them. It was an accident. You saw. Tell them you saw me do it.

DESIRE: They won't believe me.

HEARTACHE: Of course they will.

DESIRE: Just trust me okay? I can't vouch for you.

HEARTACHE: Why can't you go find the doctor and try?

DESIRE: I'm not leaving. They told me to stay with you.

HEARTACHE: I'm flattered. But I'm leaving.

DESIRE: Heartache even with accidental overdoses they think—

HEARTACHE: —I don't care what they think. Doctors' opin-
-ions never helped me. Look I'm fine. (*Reaches as far as she can towards him, supporting herself on the bed.*) Now give me my cane. I'm not leaving without it.

DESIRE: (*Stands up, holding the cane away from Heartache's reach.*) Hey, cut it out...You're not fine. You're in the hospital for an accidental overdose. I don't even know your real name but I do know you're too smart to be this careless. What happened to you? Who hurt you?

HEARTACHE: I...look it's not just that I've been hurt before, it's just that I can't...

DESIRE: Can't what?

HEARTACHE: Be with anyone. Not for real, anyway.

DESIRE: Why not?

HEARTACHE: (*Gestures at her heart.*) Because...it's broken.

DESIRE: What? Your heart? Please, everyone gets their heart... (*Makes air quotes with his hands.*) ...Broken at some point. It's just a part of life. But then you pick yourself up and move on.

HEARTACHE: Like you understand.

DESIRE: (*Reaches forward as if to touch her.*) Look, at least sit down—

HEARTACHE: (*Pulls away from Desire and clutches at her chest.*) Ow! Please don't.

DESIRE: (*Draws back, looking hurt.*) Sorry.

HEARTACHE: (*Sits.*) Desire, with my heart it's...different. My heart...my heart has a crack in it.

DESIRE: (*Sits.*) What?

HEARTACHE: A couple years ago I met someone. And I made the stupid mistake of trusting him. I trusted him with everything, even my heart. We got engaged. Then one day I came home early from work only to find him in bed with another woman.

DESIRE: What did you do?

HEARTACHE: I kicked him out the door and out of my life. But my heart couldn't take his betrayal. I had to drive myself to the emergency room and...

DESIRE: What happened?

HEARTACHE: The doctors told me in so many medical terms that the shock had cracked my heart vertically down the middle. That there was nothing they could do. That any more shock could cause my heart to break in half. I didn't want to believe them so for the past year...I've seen more doctors than I can remember. I've tried all kinds of medications whose names I can't even pronounce. I take so many pills I could run a working pharmacy out of my medicine cabinet right now. (*Beat.*) But nothing is working. It's like my body doesn't know how to not be sick. I don't even know if I can heal, I've forgotten what it feels like to be healthy, to feel normal.

DESIRE: Because no one's found the cure for a broken heart yet...

HEARTACHE: It goes further than medication. I have to protect my heart. I can't allow myself to get hurt by anyone. If I do then...then I'm afraid of what will happen to me.

DESIRE: Heartache...if losing love is what cracked your heart in the first place, then shouldn't you be exposing it to as much love as possible to mend it?

HEARTACHE: They told me not to take that chance if I wanted to see my next birthday.

DESIRE: But that's not fair to you. Trust me, if you reject love long enough you'll forget how to accept it.

HEARTACHE: Life may not be fair, but it does give you a choice. And I choose to be alone. (*Beat.*) There's so much pain in wanting to be with someone and knowing you can't because you have to heal first. How do you tell someone you like that you're broken?

DESIRE: I'm sorry.

HEARTACHE: Not your fault that I'm a mess. (*Looks at Desire.*) So, who hurt you?

DESIRE: Ex-girlfriend. But it was my fault really. I got serious too fast and I scared her away. Like, I said I love you too soon.

HEARTACHE: Oh, well it can be exciting to be in love and sometimes you just say things...

DESIRE: Not the way I did it. You know what she said after I told her I loved her?

HEARTACHE: That she had feelings bordering along the lines of a similar emotional connection but thought it a more mature decision to wait until you had known each other exclusively for six months before saying such a binding statement again?
   (*Beat. Desire is taken aback.*)
Kidding. I'm kidding. What'd she say after you said I love you?

DESIRE: Shit.

HEARTACHE: Oh...shit.

DESIRE: Yeah...

HEARTACHE: Oh...

DESIRE: Yeah, I did not expect her to react that way.

HEARTACHE: Well, they do say love is blind.

DESIRE: (*Laughs morosely.*) You can say that again.

HEARTACHE: Don't worry. I won't. (*Beat.*) So, now that we've sung kumbaya together, can I have my cane please?

DESIRE: But the doctor should be back soon—

HEARTACHE: Desire I'm not staying here like a hostage any longer. (*Leans toward him, hand outstretched.*) Cane. Now.

DESIRE: Heartache no.

HEARTACHE: Desire.

DESIRE: No.

HEARTACHE: Give it! (*Lunges for the cane. A tug-of-war begins.*)

DESIRE: Ah Heartache! Ow!

HEARTACHE: Give me my cane! If I spend one more minute of my existence here I'll go completely mad!
(*They fight. In the struggle Heartache rips off Desire's glasses and the glasses fall to the floor. Desire immediately panics and lets go of Heartache's cane, scanning the floor. Heartache holds the cane triumphantly.*)
Ah ha!

DESIRE: (*Gets on the floor on his hands and knees.*) Oh no...Where are they?!

HEARTACHE: What?

DESIRE: My glasses! Where are they?

HEARTACHE: Desire they're right...no...over to your...oh for... (*Gets on her knees and grabs the glasses, facing Desire as he turns towards her.*) Desire, they're right—(*Makes eye contact with Desire as she hands the glasses to him.*)—Here...

DESIRE: (*Takes back the glasses, unaware of the shocked expression on Heartache's face.*) Thanks. Sorry...sorry.

(*They both slowly stand up. Heartache supports herself with the bed, staring at Desire. Desire moves to put the glasses back on.*)

HEARTACHE: Wait!
   (*Desire freezes.*)
Desire. Your eyes. They're...Are you—

DESIRE: Blind? (*Unfreezes. Shrugs and nods.*) Yeah.

(*Beat. Heartache's mouth hangs open in shock.*)

HEARTACHE: Oooohhhh! How did I miss that? I mean you don't act like...

DESIRE: (*Holds up his glasses, doesn't put them back on.*) Electronic eyewear, outlines shapes and helps me pass for a non-blind individual.

HEARTACHE: Have you always been...?

DESIRE: No, it developed a few months ago. I've seen plenty of doctors myself. One doctor with thirty years of experience told me I was a complete enigma to him.

HEARTACHE: Enigma?

DESIRE: A puzzle. I had to ask him what he meant too.

HEARTACHE: So you can't see at all?

DESIRE: I can still see in my dreams, but not when I'm awake.

HEARTACHE: So you just woke up one day...

DESIRE: Sort of. It was a weird coincidence. The night before I'd told my girlfriend that I loved her.

HEARTCAHE: The one who said "shit?"

DESIRE: Yeah. When I woke up she was gone. Just a note saying she was sorry. I remember lying in bed, thinking that I was so stupid, so blind, not to see that she didn't love me back. Then...

HEARTACHE: Darkness?

DESIRE: More so panic. And explicit language. But yeah. Darkness.

HEARTACHE: Desire...

DESIRE: You can go if you want. I won't try to stop you.

(*Heartache leans on her cane and walks to the door. She hesitates, looks back at Desire, and then back at the door.*)

Act II, Scene 4

(*Guarded and Silenced are sitting on the bench outside the restaurant. Guarded is filling out a Mad Libs book. He has his medical mask and medical gloves on. Silenced has a new piece of duct tape over her mouth. She has an opened beer in one hand.*)

GUARDED: Silenced? Can you think of an adjective?
(*Silenced shakes her head and removes her tape, taking a sip of her beer.*)
Okay then. Stubborn. (*Writes the word down. Looks at Silenced.*) Still not talking to me?
(*Silenced shakes her head. She then produces an extra beer and holds it out to him. Guarded takes off his mask and sets it down. He takes the drink from her.*)
Is this root beer?

SILENCED: No. Just beer.

GUARDED: Oh no thanks. (*Hands the beer back.*) I don't drink.

SILENCED: (*In disbelief.*) Are you Mormon?

GUARDED: (*Throws up his hands, forgetting to put his mask back on.*) Why do people always assume that? No, I'm not. I'm just careful.

SILENCED: I don't trust someone that doesn't drink.

GUARDED: And I don't trust anyone who does.

SILENCED: Touché. (*Takes a huge sip of her beer.*)

GUARDED: Geez how many of those have you had?
(*Silenced holds up six fingers.*)
What? How are you still awake?
(*Silenced shrugs, taking a bag of snacks out of her purse. Simon enters from offstage, carrying his items and looking around.*)

SIMON: (*Notices Silenced and Guarded.*) Oops! Sorry, wrong scene. (*Exits.*)

GUARDED: (*Looking after him in shock.*) Why is he...?

SILENCED: No idea. (*Put the duct tape back over her mouth.*)

GUARDED: Huh. (*Looks at his Mad Libs book. Beat.*) Okay I need an adjective and a noun, back-to-back.
(*Silenced reaches over and takes Guarded's Mad Libs book and pencil from him, giving him the bag of snacks to hold. Guarded takes off his gloves, only to reveal a second pair of gloves underneath. He sprays them with the air disinfectant spray. Silenced writes in her answers. Just as Guarded is about to take reach into the snack bag, Silenced takes it back from him, exchanging the Mad Libs book and pencil for her bag of snacks. Guarded looks at what Silenced has written.*)
Adjective, evil. Noun, kiss. Evil kiss? (*Gives her a look.*) Very funny. I wasn't joking when I said that. A kiss is bad news.
(*Silenced crosses her arms and shakes her head.*)
Yes, it is. Even if you don't get sick from it, a kiss will still trap you.

SILENCED: (*Takes off her duct tape in frustration and sticks it in her purse.*) This is probably the six beers I've had talking but...trap you? Kissing isn't supposed to be a torture chamber. It's romantic.

GUARDED: Kissing isn't romantic, it's binding. There's no way I'm gonna let some kiss infect or trap me.

SILENCED: Come on, kissing isn't that bad. Not if you do it with a right person.

GUARDED: And just how are you supposed to know if it's the right person before it's too late? Before they infect you with love? Trap you?

SILENCED: Not "THE" right person, I said "A" right person. There are lots of great people you could end up with. And as far as knowing if they're right or not I have no clue. But I guess you try to build up a tolerance to love until you find A right person.

GUARDED: Love is too powerful. You can't build up a tolerance to it.

SILENCED: I think if you expose yourself to it then you can fight it off more easily. Maybe kissing is, ironically, a kind of immunization. I mean I'm no doctor but isn't that how shots work? You're exposed to the germs so your body can fight them off?

GUARDED: Fighting it once was more than enough for me.

SILENCED: What?

GUARDED: Nothing.

SILENCED: No you said...

GUARDED: Drop it please.

SILENCED: (*Starts as if she's just remembered something.*)
Wait a minute...

GUARDED: Oh no.

SILENCED: I remember hearing you mention to Dr. Adams
that you were once hospitalized. It wasn't because you got...

GUARDED: Yeah, I got infected pretty badly.

SILENCED: How did you catch it?

GUARDED: From this girl I knew.

SILENCED: Who was she?

GUARDED: My best friend.

SILENCED: Oh, I'm so sorry.

GUARDED: It's okay I guess. Anyway, you know the drill.
Boy meets girl. Boy falls deeply in love with girl, but in the end
girl can't commit because it's too...complicated for her. So girl
breaks up with boy. But I was already infected. (*Beat.*) I spent
three days in the ICU. Nothing but white walls and IV drips
and more needles. I hate hospitals. I don't ever want to go
back. And that means I'll do whatever I can to make sure I
don't get sick with love again.

SILENCED: But you obviously got better.

GUARDED: At a price. I learned the hard way that I'm easily susceptible to love. I can't take that risk again.

SILENCED: (*Beat. Checks her phone.*) Hey, if it makes you feel any better, you've kept your mask off for way longer than a minute. I think our bet still stands.

GUARDED: Oh. (*Surprised. Picks his mask back up, laughing slightly.*) I guess I did. Looks like you owe me everything in your wallet.

SILENCED: (*Takes out her wallet.*) Don't be too sure. (*Opens her wallet and shakes it upside down. Nothing falls out.*)

GUARDED: You never had anything in it did you?

SILENCED: Nope!

GUARDED: (*Slowly claps his hands.*) Very good.

SILENCED: (*Gives a little bow.*) Thank you. Thank you.

GUARDED: Hey, for the record, or off the record if you prefer, I like the talking version of you better.

SILENCED: And I like the unmasked version of you better.

GUARDED: Thanks, Silenced. (*Turns towards the restaurant entrance.*) Wanna see if our table's ready?

SILENCED: Sure. One sec. (*Rummages around in her purse.*)

GUARDED: Oh right you gotta put your tape back on. I guess I should thank you for keeping it off for so long. At least now we'll have something great to talk about at next week's session—

SILENCED: (*Takes out an empty plastic bag/wrap. Turns to Guarded, who is facing away from her.*) Hey, before I do that...

(*Guarded turns to face her. Silenced uses the small plastic bag/wrap as a barrier between her and Guarded to kiss him. They pull apart.*)

HOST: (*Calls from offstage.*) Table for Guarded?

GUARDED: That's us.

(*They walk offstage together.*)

Act II, Scene 5

(Grief and Dependence are seated in Heartache's car. Dependence is in the driver's seat. Grief is in the passenger seat. He has his handcuffed hand placed near Dependence so she can drive easier and is covering his eyes with his free hand.)

DEPENDENCE: Grief.

GRIEF: *(Shakes his head.)* Uh. Uh.

DEPENDENCE: Grief.

GRIEF: Nope.

DEPENDENCE: Grief. We're here. You can look now.

GRIEF: *(Takes his hand off of his eyes. Sighs with relief.)* Oh.
     (Grief and Dependence try to get out of the car on their own sides, but they pull each other in opposite directions.)
You got me into this mess, we're getting out on my side.

DEPENDENCE: And I got us here without an accident, no thanks to you.

GRIEF: Fine! We'll settle this the old-fashioned way. *(Turns to Dependence and they play rock paper scissors. Grief plays rock. Dependence plays scissors.)* Haha!

     (Dependence and Grief struggle to get out on the passenger side together, finally succeeding after much trial and error.)

DEPENDENCE: (*Looking around.*) Think we'll find her here?

GRIEF: She wasn't at the park or coffee shop. This is the last place I can think of to look for her.

DEPENDENCE: A fountain?

GRIEF: We came here after the doctor broke the bad news to her. Haven't been here in forever.

DEPENDENCE: Maybe Heartache and Desire are having more luck than we are.

GRIEF: Maybe.

(*Simon enters from offstage carrying his stuff and Dependence's jacket.*)

SIMON: Oh there you are. Been looking all over the play for you. (*Hands Dependence's jacket to her.*) Here.

(*Dependence and Grief stare after Simon as he exits.*)

GRIEF: Was that—

DEPENDENCE: —It's best not to question it.

GRIEF: (*Looks at Dependence's jacket and points to it.*) But hey! He brought your jacket. Quick see if the key is there. Hurry!

DEPENDENCE: (*Turns all the pockets inside out.*) It's not here.

GRIEF: (*Looking behind her.*) But Caitlin is.

DEPENDENCE: (*Turns around as Grief spins her in the opposite direction.*) What?

(*The audience sees that Caitlin's chair has reappeared onstage.*)

GRIEF: Caitlin! Thank goodness we found you. If we leave now we can still make it to the art exhibit. Caitlin come on we have to go. Please. (*Beat.*) Caitlin?

DEPENDENCE: What's wrong?

GRIEF: She doesn't want to come with me. This has never happened before.

DEPENDENCE: Maybe she has a reason for it.

GRIEF: (*Steps towards Caitlin's chair.*) Caitlin, if you're mad about me wanting to move, then don't worry. I won't. Things can stay the same. Just as they were. Caitlin?

DEPENDENCE: (*Pulls on the handcuffs to hold Grief back.*) Grief? I don't think she wants to go with you.

GRIEF: (*Pulls forward against Dependence's hold.*) Yes she does, she's just confused. Caitlin please I'm so sorry I left you. I promise I won't do it again. I love you Caitlin. I need you. Caitlin? (*Panics.*) Caitlin don't leave me! Please! (*Launches himself towards Caitlin's chair, bringing Dependence along with him.*)

DEPENDENCE: Ow Grief. Stop it! (*Pulls back on the handcuffs, turning him towards her.*) Who says you get to choose if she stays? Newsflash. You don't get to decide if the people you love leave or not. When my dad got sick I didn't get to choose. No matter how much you love someone you can't make them stay. I know because my love wasn't enough to keep him alive.

(*Beat.*)

GRIEF: I didn't know you'd lost someone.

DEPENDENCE: Most people don't.

GRIEF: I'm sorry. (*Beat.*) And I'm sorry you have to see me like this.

DEPENDENCE: Never apologize for being human.

GRIEF: I won't. (*Looks at Caitlin's chair hopelessly.*) But what about Caitlin? How can I reason with her?

DEPENDENCE: You can't.

GRIEF: What?

DEPENDENCE: Grief, look at Caitlin. I mean really look at her. (*Gestures towards Caitlin's chair.*) Her being here of all places, becoming distant, leaving you all those times. Don't you see? She obviously needs to move on. Why can't you?

GRIEF: Because she's still here! How can I move on if she won't leave me?

DEPENDENCE: Because you won't let her!

> (*Grief opens his mouth to speak and then closes it, turning his head.*)

(*Speaks gently.*) Grief, I obviously can't speak for Caitlin, but from the little you've told me it seems like she needs to leave, but...feels compelled to stay with you?

> (*Beat. Grief looks at Caitlin's chair longingly.*)

Grief?

GRIEF: How can you let someone go when you've already spent so much of your life with them? It just doesn't feel natural.

DEPENDENCE: I don't know. I guess you just do it.

GRIEF: (*Continues to look at Caitlin's chair.*) How?

> (*Both are silent. Grief stares at Caitlin's chair while Dependence stares at their handcuffed hands. Depen--dence suddenly reaches into her bra or pocket and takes out the key to the handcuffs. She unlocks them and takes out her hand, leaving Grief's hand in the cuffs.*)

DEPENDENCE: Like this.

GRIEF: You mean you've had the key the whole time...?

DEPENDENCE: Yeah. I'm sorry...I just didn't want to be alone tonight...I understand if you never want to speak to me again. I think I'd better go. (*Starts to leave, and then feels her wrist like she's forgotten something. Realizes that her handcuffs are still on Grief's wrist and points to them.*) You can keep those I...I'm sure I have an extra pair at home somewhere. (*Gives Grief a regretful look and starts to walk offstage.*)

(*Grief removes the handcuffs from his wrist, holding them in one of his hands. He looks at Caitlin's chair and then back at Dependence and then back at the chair, as if waiting for something. Then he nods at the chair and goes after Dependence.*)

GRIEF: Hey wait! Um...
(*Dependence turns around.*)
You know you don't have to be alone tonight. Caitlin says she'd prefer to stay here where it's peaceful...but she thinks we might enjoy the exhibit...That is, if you'd like to go with me?

DEPENDENCE: (*Looks over at Caitlin's chair.*) You're sure Caitlin won't mind?

GRIEF: I...I think she'll be okay...I mean...As long as you're okay with it... (*Holds out his free hand towards Dependence.*)

DEPENDENCE: (*Hesitates, and then slowly takes his hand.*) Thanks. You know...I'd like that.

(*Grief and Dependence smile at each other, each a little lighter.*)

Act II, Scene 6

(*Heartache and Desire are both sitting on Heartache's hospital bed, leaning against each other, fast asleep. Desire's glasses are in his hands. Desire wakes up, looks around, and then gently nudges Heartache awake.*)

DESIRE: Hey...sorry. What time is it?

HEARTACHE: (*Looks at the wall.*) The clock says it's about 1:40...am.

DESIRE: It's late.

HEARTACHE: Think they'll let me go in the morning?

DESIRE: I don't really know how it works...but I don't see why not.

HEARTACHE: Pun intended?

DESIRE: A little.

(*Beat.*)

HEARTACHE: Aren't you going to ask?

DESIRE: Ask what?

HEARTACHE: Why I stayed?

DESIRE: Why did you?

HEARTACHE: Because when I overdosed you stayed with me first.

DESIRE: Whoa, careful. You're starting to sound romantic.

HEARTACHE: Don't worry. I won't make a habit of it.

DESIRE: (*Stands up, leaving his glasses on the bed, and carefully walks a couple paces away from Heartache.*) I lied to you, earlier.

HEARTACHE: What?

DESIRE: (*Turns around to look at Heartache.*) I lied when I said I didn't know your real name, but I heard the doctor say it before you came to.

HEARTACHE: Oh.

DESIRE: I'm sorry. I know we're only supposed to use aliases for the group therapy but—

HEARTACHE: No, it's okay. I think we're way past formali--ties at this point.

DESIRE: It's a pretty name.

HEARTACHE: Thanks. I've always liked it. Although I've enjoyed being Heartache too.

DESIRE: Enough to change it?

HEARTACHE: (*Laughs.*) Not that much.

DESIRE: (*Looks up, listening to music that is being played over the hospital loudspeakers.*) They must play this music for the night staff.

HEARTACHE: It's nice. Like something you'd dance to.

DESIRE: Would it be weird if I asked you to dance now?

HEARTACHE: I don't know. Ask me.

DESIRE: Would you like to dance?

HEARTACHE: I thought you didn't dance.

DESIRE: Well, one dance can't hurt me. Probably won't cure me either, but I don't mind.

HEARTACHE: (*Enjoying teasing Desire.*) I just overdosed. I don't know if I have the strength to stand.

DESIRE: We can hold each other up. I won't let you fall.

HEARTACHE: Well...okay. One condition. You tell me your name.

DESIRE: I guess I do have an unfair advantage in knowing yours. It's— (*Reaches out, finds Heartache's shoulder, and then leans down to whisper into Heartache's ear. Straightens back up, taking a step back.*)

HEARTACHE: Thank you.

DESIRE: (*Extends his hand towards Heartache.*) May I have this dance, Odette?

HEARTACHE: (*Leaves her cane on the bed. Takes Desire's hand.*) I'd be delighted, Andrew.

Act II, Scene 7

(*Unrequited Love and Lost have finished searching around the tree, with no luck.*)

UNREQUITED LOVE: (*Sits on the ground, disappointed at not finding Lost's heart.*) I'm sorry Lost. I'm completely empty-handed.

LOST: (*Sits on the ground next to her, keeping several inches between them.*) The search was futile, but it was considerate of you to make the effort. I mean it's more than anyone else has ever done. (*Beat.*) You okay? You seem...unusually despond- -ent.

UNREQUITED LOVE: Yeah I'm okay. (*Beat.*) Lost, can I ask you something?

LOST: Sure.

UNREQUITED LOVE: Besides your heart, how badly were you injured in the accident?

LOST: Not that badly. I was lucky compared to most people. It made me want to help others.

UNREQUITED LOVE: Is that why you design pacemakers and such?

LOST: I hadn't thought about it specifically, but...I think I do it because I want to make people feel whole again. No one wants to go walking around without a functional heartbeat.

UNREQUITED LOVE: Lost? If you can't experience love, then what do you feel every day?
> (*Beat. Lost doesn't respond. Unrequited Love tries to assure Lost with her smile.*)

Anything you say won't be as stupid as me carting around those I can't let go of.
> (*Long beat. Lost looks away.*)

I'll tell you how I feel. Some days my body feels empty and I feel like an idiot. To care for someone with every inch of your soul, and then find out they couldn't care less about you... It's like being slowly stabbed in the chest by someone who enjoys murdering the innocent.

LOST: But you always seem so happy.

UNREQUITED LOVE: There's only so much you can't feel.

LOST: (*Nods.*) Some days I feel empty too.
> (*Beat. He nudges Unrequited Love, trying to make her smile.*)

Okay, more like every day.
> (*Unrequited Love smiles.*)

Hey, you know, when I design hearts, I have to make sure that the proper amount of blood will flow through the manufactured valves with each heartbeat. But, I have to be careful because the heart can only hold so much, or else you run the risk of heart failure. Maybe these guys are taking up space in your heart in a similar way. And the sooner you realize that relationships with them weren't meant to be, the sooner you can make room for what is... (*Surprised by his own words.*) Sorry, I don't know where that came from.

UNREQUITED LOVE: Maybe from your heart.

LOST: But...I don't have a heart.

UNREQUITED LOVE: I meant metaphorically.

LOST: Oh.

(*Beat.*)

UNREQUITED LOVE: Geez it's freezing out. My fingertips are numb.

LOST: Mine too. (*Checks his watch.*) Oh wow it's late. I'd better get you back. I've already taken up too much of your time.

(*Lost stands up, and then takes Unrequited Love's hands, helping her stand up.*)

UNREQUITED LOVE: It's okay. I had fun.

LOST: Me too.

(*Beat. Looks into Unrequited Love's eyes. They are still holding each other's hands.*)

UNREQUITED LOVE: What?

LOST: Oh nothing, just...your eyes. They're really nice.

UNREQUITED LOVE: Oh. Thank you.

(*Lost looks behind Unrequited Love and sees that the car is empty. Simon is gone.*)

LOST: Oh no.

UNREQUITED LOVE: What?

(*Lost hurries over to the car and opens the door. Unrequited Love freezes in place.*)

LOST: Where's Simon? Oh no, please don't tell me he sleepwalked away from here. (*Looks through the car, checking under the seats.*) Simon? (*Shuts the car door and looks around. Notices Unrequited Love is still frozen in place.*) Alright, we didn't leave him alone for that long, so he probably walked back up the street that way so if we... (*Notices that she isn't budging.*) Unrequited Love?

UNREQUITED LOVE: You won't find him.

LOST: (*Approaches her.*) What? Where's Simon?

UNREQUITED LOVE: I...I let him go.

LOST: (*Taken aback.*) Really?

UNREQUITED LOVE: Yeah.

LOST: Are you okay?

UNREQUITED LOVE: I don't know.

LOST: Are you...relieved that he's gone?

UNREQUITED LOVE: Yeah, but I still have to deal with

all the other days of the week. (*Motions to the car. The audience sees that the wagon is still in the backseat.*)

LOST: Something tells me you're gonna to be okay.

UNREQUITED LOVE: Thanks. What about you?

LOST: Well, someday I'll find my heart. And then I'll try to keep better track of it.

UNREQUITED LOVE: Once you find it you'll have to get re-acquainted with it.

LOST: That's gonna take some time.

UNREQUITED LOVE: If it's okay with you, I could help. (*Wraps her arms around herself.*) When you find it I mean.

LOST: (*Puzzled by her actions.*) What are you doing?

UNREQUITED LOVE: I'm hugging myself. It's comforting and it makes me feel safe. (*Notices his expression.*) You don't really get that, do you?

LOST: I...

UNREQUITED LOVE: (*Holds up her hand.*) I know. I know. Missing heart and all. (*Beat.*) Lost? When was the last time someone hugged you?

LOST: I can't remember, I...

UNREQUITED LOVE: (*Starts as if she's had an idea.*) Here.

(*Unrequited Love steps forward and wraps her arms around Lost in a hug. Lost stiffens a bit, thrown off by this sudden display of affection. He keeps his arms outstretched straight in front of him, not hugging her back, unsure of what to do.*)

LOST: Um...How do you—?

UNREQUITED LOVE: Just give it a second. It'll come back to you.
   (*Beat. Lost slowly wraps his arms around her, returning the hug.*)
Does this help?

LOST: I still don't understand, but I do feel...safe.

   (*The audience hears the soft sound of a heartbeat, "Thump."*)

UNREQUITED LOVE: Well, that's a start.

   (*The audience hears the louder sound of a heartbeat, "Thump."*)

   (*Unrequited Love and Lost pull away from each other, but they are still standing close together. Their eyes meet. Lost's hand goes to the left side of his chest as he stares at Unrequited Love. They hold each other's gaze, not saying anything. The audience hears multiple sounds of a heartbeat in slow succession, "Thump, thump, thump, thump, thump, thump, thump, thump..."*)

LOST AND FOUND

Character Property List

Dependence
- Pair of fuzzy handcuffs
- Jacket with pockets
- Cell phone

Desire
- Sunglasses

Grief
- Collapsible chair
- Cell phone

Guarded
- Packet of antiviral masks
- Packet of medical gloves
- Tiny air disinfectant spray
- Mad-Libs book

Heartache
- Curved, wooden walking cane
- Medicine bottle filled with pills
- Purse
- Car keys
- Hospital gown
- Cell phone

Lost
- Watch
- Tie-able shoes
- A wallet with money inside it

Silenced
- A roll of duct/medical/sports tape
- Purse
- Empty wallet
- Plastic bag of snacks
- Empty plastic bag/wrap
- 6-Pack of Beers
- Cell Phone

Simon
- Clipboard
- Miscellaneous items for wagon interior (i.e. Rubik's cube, adult magazine, etc.)
- Monopoly money
- Sleep mask
- Concession stand items
- Cell phone

Unrequited Love
- Classic Red Metal Wagon
- Cell phone

Stage Property List

- 9 Folding chairs
- Written note from Caitlin: "Went to get some air. Love Caitlin."
- Bench
- Small rug with side fringe
- Door within frame
- Bartender bar
- 2 Bar glasses
- 1 Cosmopolitan glass
- 2 Restaurant glasses
- Liquor bottle
- Shot glass
- Sprite – Gin and Tonic
- Apple juice – Jameson on The Rocks
- Lemonade
- Ice

Sound Effects

Page 10, Cell phone ringtone
Page 17, Car engine starting up
Page 17, Love song
Page 18, Car engine starting up
Page 18, Love song
Page 35, Recently released dance song
Page 89, A song you could dance to
Page 96, Heartbeat

Acknowledgements

Thank you to Dr. Michelle Miller-Day for your amazing guidance, encouragement, and for giving this play (and its author) a chance.

Thank you to Deb Marley for your vision, strength, and leadership in directing a beautiful workshop production of *Lost and Found.*

Thank you to Dr. Andrea Weber for going above and beyond in your support for this play.

Thank you to Dr. Jocelyn Buckner for your valuable advice.

Thank you to Dr. Samantha Dorros for you lecture on the theory of uncertainty reduction; it formed the basis for this play.

Thank you to the original cast of the workshop performance of *Lost and Found.* Your hard work, dedication to your craft, and the spirit you brought to each character is inspiring.

Thank you to the original cast of the workshop reading of *Lost and Found.* You brought the play and its characters to life.

Thank you to Parker Danowski for your wonderful review.

Thank you to Rick Adams for your insight & wisdom.

Thank you to Sbav & Co for your exquisite cover design.

A special thank you to my parents, friends, & extended family for your endless support and love. To those who attended the performances, a HUGE thank you.

Thank you to everyone who reads, performs, produces, and/or watches this play. I hope you enjoy the experience.

About the Author

Alyssa Ahle is a playwright and author whose work has been published in the anthology book series *America's Emerging Literary Fiction Writers: California; America's Emerging Science Fiction Writers: Pacific Region; California's Emerging Writers: An Anthology of Fiction* by Z Publishing House. Her work has also appeared in Germ Magazine and The Calliope Art & Literary Magazine. She co-produced her full-length stage play, *Lost and Found,* at the Chance Theater in November of 2017. As a writer, she aspires to draw attention to the beauty and humor of life.